MICHAEL DAHL PRESENTS

SCREAMS IN SPACE 4D

END USER

BY STEVE BREZENOFF
ILLUSTRATED BY JUAN CALLE

STONE ARCH BOOKS
a capstone imprint

Michael Dahl Presents is published by Stone Arch Books,
A Capstone Imprint
1710 Roe Crest Drive
North Mankato, Minnesota 56003
www.capstonepub.com

Library of Congress Cataloging-in-Publication Data is available on the Library of Congress website.
ISBN: 978-1-4965-8335-2 (library hardcover)
ISBN: 978-1-4965-8337-6 (ebook PDF)

Summary: Twelve-year-old twins Raz and Kiley are headed underground, along with everyone else
aboard the asteroid station. Their home is about to pass through a band of deadly space radiation,
and in the lower level they'll be safe. But soon the kids spot ghostly figures flickering in the halls.
Rooms suddenly appear abandoned and run-down. Is it just a minor glitch in the computer's
holographic system, as the adults claim, or is something more sinister stirring? Download the
Capstone 4D app to access a variety of bonus content.

Printed and bound in the USA.
PA70

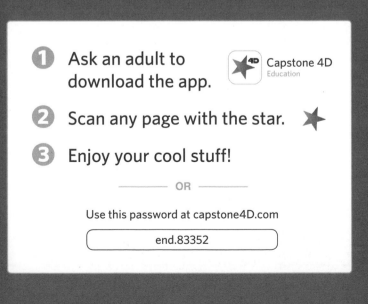

1. Ask an adult to download the app.

Capstone 4D
Education

2. Scan any page with the star.

3. Enjoy your cool stuff!

— OR —

Use this password at capstone4D.com

end.83352

MICHAEL
DAHL
PRESENTS

Michael Dahl has written about werewolves, magicians, and superheroes. He loves funny books, scary books, and mysterious books. Every Michael Dahl Presents book is chosen by Michael himself and written by an author he loves. The books are about favorite subjects like monster aliens, haunted houses, farting pigs, or magical powers that go haywire. Read on!

INTO THE DARK . . .

When I look at the night sky, I wonder—does scary stuff happen up there just as it does here on Earth? Sounds can't travel through outer space because there's no air. So if frightened people were out there, we'd never even hear their screams. I wonder . . .

In *End User*, the science station on asteroid 2035 RAXQ is passing through a toxic radiation belt. The crew, including young friends Raz, Kiley, and Donnell, will wait out the danger in the deep inner tunnels of the space rock. The station computer is also supposed to help keep the humans alive and well. But it soon develops a new, deadlier plan.

Michael Dahl

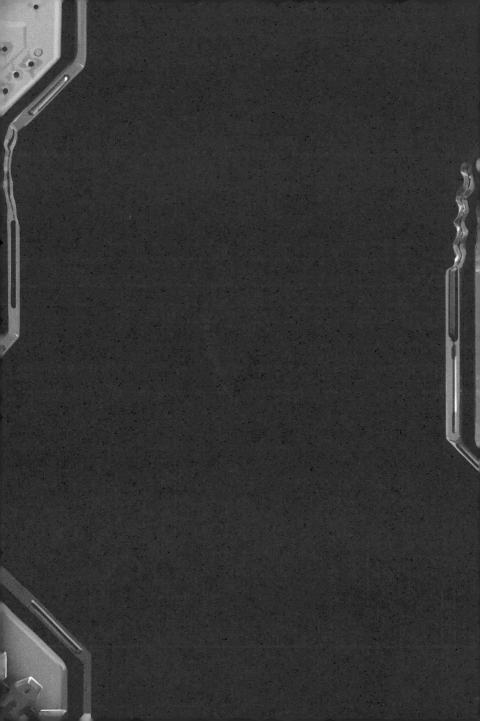

The asteroid known officially as 2035 RAXQ moved in a wide orbit around the sun, along with thousands of other asteroids. On the surface of 2035 RAXQ sat a building of metal and glass.

This was Science Station: Rock, and the building's yellow electric lights made 2035 RAXQ the coziest-looking asteroid in the asteroid belt. In fact, three of the station's youngest residents sat together in the lounge and felt very cozy indeed.

"I'm starving," said twelve-year-old Raz Mack.

"Me too," his twin sister, Kiley, said.

Raz and Kiley were lying on their backs and staring through the high glass ceiling. The inky sky was speckled with glittering, diamond-like stars. Up toward the left, Jupiter glowed a ghostly white, its orange stripes barely visible.

Donnell Prince straightened up in his chair. He was a year older than the twins and the only other child on the station. He sniffed the air.

"Supper is ready," he said. "*Mmm.* Smells like rations seven through twelve."

"Seven through twelve," Kiley said, tapping her chin. "Let's see. That would be . . . corn on the cob . . ."

"With butter," added Raz.

"Plus green beans and grilled chicken fillets?" Kiley continued.

Donnell nodded. "And eleven and twelve," he said. "Sorbet and vitamin water."

"Of course," Kiley said, getting to her feet. "What meal would be complete without vitamin water?"

Raz stood up beside her. "Just once I'd like ration nineteen."

"I don't think it really exists," Donnell said.

Kiley shot him an ice-cold glare. "Don't you dare shatter our hopes of one day having chocolate milk!" she said.

The two boys laughed as they all hurried to the mess hall for supper.

✦ ✦ ✦

"There you three are! I just sent Jeeves to fetch you," said Jenn Prince.

Jenn was Donnell's mom and one of the few adults on the station who was not a scientist. Still, everyone had a role to fill, and Jenn acted as the kids' tutor.

Raz stopped in front of the dinner table. He straightened his back and clasped his hands as he launched into his Jeeves impression. "I say, young gentlemen and lady," he said, in a posh British accent. "The hour to *sup* has arrived. *Make haste* to the dining room."

Raz bowed to the laughter of his friends. He had even impressed the other adults. Skot Prince, Donnell's father and head of the artificial intelligence division, clapped. Dr. Poli Mack, the twins' mother and head of elemental research, gave a rare smile.

Dr. Mack had dreamed up Science Station: Rock as a graduate student back on Earth. It had taken years of work to make the station a reality.

The Rock still needed supplies from their home planet, but Dr. Mack hoped to one day build a community that could take care of itself. She imagined creating the first human-controlled asteroid. It would have homes, schools, farms, and science stations. And it'd have thrusters so the whole asteroid could be piloted like a starship throughout the galaxy.

Anyway, that was the dream, and it was a dream shared by everyone aboard the Rock. Usually the station held about thirty people. But most of the staff were back on Earth for the next four weeks to present research, pick up supplies, and visit family. That left only the Macks and the Princes aboard.

Raz didn't mind, though. The station wasn't as busy now, and he liked having some relaxed time with his mom. He gave another bow to the small group.

Just then a blue light flickered beside the table. An instant later, a blue-tinted man appeared. He had a thin mustache, stiff posture, and his hands were folded neatly in front of him.

The man frowned at Raz. "I see the children have found their own way to supper," he said.

"Hi, Jeeves," Raz said, smiling nervously. "Sorry about the impression. I was just kidding around."

Jeeves held his nose up high. "No apology necessary, Master Raz," he said. "End-user satisfaction is my main concern. I cannot be offended—no matter how insulting or bad the impression is."

Raz felt his cheeks grow warm as he slid into his seat.

The holographic butler turned toward Jenn. "Will there be anything else, Ms. Prince?"

"No, Jeeves," Jenn said, smiling. "Thank you."

Jeeves was a hologram. His body was a 3D image created by lights, and his mind was made up of digital computer code. Yet the crew had a hard time treating Jeeves as anything other than a real, human butler.

In fact, all the holograms on board felt like actual people to the station staff. There were several, and each had a different role and a different personality.

"Very good," Jeeves said, bowing to Jenn. "Please fill out an end-user satisfaction report at your earliest convenience. I'll switch off." And just like that, he flickered out of existence.

"I'll have to poke around the Jeeves program," Skot said as everyone else dug into their meals. "He shouldn't have said Raz's joke was insulting. That's a touch too human, I think."

Skot Prince had designed the station's computer systems with his mentor, Dr. Harlan Moors. He worked on the computer so much that he had even nicknamed it "Art." It was short for "artificial intelligence." Skot was the only one who treated the holographic people like computer programs.

"Aw, Dad," Donnell said. "Give the old fellow a break."

"He's not an old fellow," Skot said. "He's not even a he."

"Maybe Dr. Moors can take a look at the program when he arrives," Jenn said.

"If anyone can get to the bottom of Art's attitude problem, he can," Skot said. "But we won't bother Dr. Moors with any station issues until later. He will have had a long and tiring trip, I'm sure."

Harlan Moors had helped build the Rock
fifteen years ago. After it was finished, he had
left to live on Jupiter Station. Now he was
finally making the trip back to visit his old
home. His shuttle was scheduled to arrive in
the lower level docking bay very early the next
morning—because something else would be
happening later that day.

"That reminds me," Dr. Mack said. "Better set
an alarm. Abigail!"

The blue light flickered again, and Abigail
appeared. She was another blue-tinted hologram,
and she acted as Dr. Mack's personal assistant.

"Right here, Doctor!" Abigail said, chipper
as can be. She held a holographic notepad and
old-fashioned pen.

"Abigail," Dr. Mack said, "please set all crew
members' alarms to five hundred hours tomorrow."

"Setting—" Abigail began, but she was drowned out by three loud, complaining voices.

"Five in the morning?" Kiley said, stunned.

"Yes," Dr. Mack replied. "As you well know, we all have to move to the station's lower level for the next few weeks until we've passed through the radiation band. We need to be down there before nine a.m., and I don't want to cut it close."

Abigail had discovered the narrow band of radiation a month ago. It could be dangerous to humans, and the asteroid's orbit would take them right through it. All space-traveling ships were protected against such radiation, but the Rock didn't have the expensive shielding. Abigail had promised Dr. Mack, though, that everyone would be safe in the deep corridors of the station's lower level.

"We're near the band *already*?" Raz said.

Raz had been dreading the move. He'd never been to the lower level, but he could imagine it. They'd be under hundreds of meters of solid rock, without even a glimmer of starlight.

Not to mention the fact that they'd be passing through a radiation band. Raz knew strong space radiation could kill human cells. That would lead to vomiting, burning skin blisters, organ failure . . . and death. What if going below wasn't enough to protect them?

"I guess time flies when you're having fun," Jenn said. She patted Raz's shoulder.

"Or when you're terrified," Raz whispered.

"That'll be all, Abigail," Dr. Mack said.

The assistant smiled and said, "Please fill out an end-user satisfaction report—you know, when you can!" She flickered away.

"I better get moving," Skot said, pushing back his chair. "I still need to finish a few things tonight so the upper floors are ready to enter the radiation band."

"What do you have to do, Dad?" Donnell asked. "Maybe I can help?"

"Thanks, but you know that Art's systems are off-limits to you kids," Skot replied. "I just need to transfer all main station controls to the lower level and set them to manual. If the radiation affects Art, I'd hate for life support to suddenly go haywire."

"Oh, but could you please leave the holograms online?" Dr. Mack said as she stabbed a green bean on her plate. "I'll have plenty for Abigail to do up here while we're down there."

Skot nodded and left the mess hall. The door closed behind him with a soft whoosh.

"As for you three," Jenn said, looking at the kids, "you had better get to bed early. Tomorrow is likely to be a very long day."

"Aw, Mom!" Donnell said.

"Yeah, it's not even nineteen hundred hours," Raz added. Beside him, Kiley nodded.

"And with all your goofing around, it'll take you three at least an hour to get into bed," Jenn said. "I want you to have time for homework too."

"Fine," Donnell said with a sigh.

After finishing their sorbet, Raz, Kiley, and Donnell got up from the table. They took their dishes to the cleaning station. Ship robots would do the rest. After all, end-user satisfaction was their main concern.

"I've never been down here," Raz said. He could hear the clanking of his teeth as he shivered. He wasn't sure if he was cold or just terrified.

"Me neither," his sister said. "But you'll be OK. It's safe."

Kiley held his hand. Though they were twins, Kiley's height and a five-minute head start in life made her feel more like a big sister to Raz.

It was six a.m. The Prince and Mack families stood together in a corridor with a tall, rounded ceiling. The corridor led into the lower level.

Raz stared down into the darkness ahead of them.

A *boom* echoed from behind. Raz jumped.

"It's OK," Kiley said, giving his hand an extra squeeze. "It's just the door closing."

Raz turned and watched Skot at the yellow door. It was as thick, huge, and heavy-looking as the door of an old bank vault. Skot turned the large wheel to lock and seal the door.

"Well, that's that," Skot said. "Down we go."

"No turning back now," Raz whispered.

"Not that you'd want to," Donnell said loudly. "The air up there will be poison in a couple hours. One second of it and you'd be—" The boy grabbed his throat and rolled back his eyes.

"Cut it out, Donnell," Kiley said.

Donnell laughed as they continued on. The corridor sloped gradually into the lowest level of the station. The walls around them were polished metal. It was the body of the asteroid itself. Though the hallway was lit, the red light was dim.

"Why is it so cold?" Donnell said. He walked behind the twins and swung his flashlight left and right, up and down.

"Environmental controls are set at the lowest setting," Dr. Mack answered from the back of the group. "Since these corridors are rarely used, they don't need to be heated much above freezing. It saves energy."

Raz nervously watched Donnell's flashlight beam as it swept across the corridor. He half believed it would reveal a terrifying alien, clinging to the ceiling, ready to devour them for breakfast.

Raz stopped walking. He knelt and fiddled with his shoelaces, pretending to tie them. He didn't want to be at the front of the group anymore. Kiley paused next to him.

Donnell passed the twins. "Wow," he said, turning back to shine the flashlight on Raz. "I thought Kiley tied your shoes for you."

"Whatever," Kiley said. "Ignore him, Raz."

"I'm fine," Raz snapped. He didn't like feeling afraid, and he didn't like needing his sister's help so often.

"Don't dally, you two," Dr. Mack said as the adults walked by. Dr. Mack held the only other flashlight, so Raz quickly got to his feet. He didn't want to be left in the dark.

"Isn't there an elevator from upper to lower engineering? Why couldn't we just take that?" Kiley asked.

"I shut it down," Skot called over his shoulder. "It's hard to know what effect the radiation might have on Art and the ship's systems. There's no telling what electronics might malfunction."

"And a falling elevator isn't a great place to find out," Raz said with a sigh. Sometimes all he could see were the dangers aboard the station.

The group's footsteps echoed along the rock walls. The noise bounced down the hallway and back again. Every step Raz took rang in his ears. It was starting to give him a headache.

"It's not much farther now," Skot said as Jenn and Dr. Mack disappeared around a bend. Skot followed them around the curve.

Then someone screamed.

"What was that?" Raz said. He held tightly to his sister's arm as Donnell ran ahead.

Kiley started running too. Raz had no choice but to go with her. It was either that or stand there alone with no flashlight.

"What happened?" Donnell said as the kids turned the corner.

Jenn was sitting on the floor. Skot knelt beside her, with an arm around her shoulders. Raz's mom stood over them.

"Is everything OK?" Raz asked.

"Oh, it's nothing," Jenn said, waving a hand. "I'm so embarrassed."

"She was just startled, that's all. She thought she saw something," Dr. Mack said.

"Some*one*," Jenn corrected her. "One of the holograms, I guess."

"Down here?" Skot said. "Huh. That's odd."

"Why is that odd?" Donnell asked.

"Well, there *are* projectors everywhere, even in this corridor," Skot replied. "The holograms can appear almost anywhere on the station. But only when called."

"I certainly didn't call a hologram," Jenn said.

"The whole place has microphones," Skot said. He looked up at the rounded ceiling. "Even if you said something *close* to a hologram call—"

"I didn't say anything!" Jenn insisted.

The group stood silently around her, their frightened mother, teacher, wife, and friend. Jenn looked past them, back up the corridor, and her face went white. Her mouth fell open.

Raz turned and looked. Just a few paces behind them, wispy and half invisible, stood a man.

His jaw was dropped low and crooked, clinging to his upper lip with only a few threads of sticky spittle. His nose was misshapen. One eye was closed, and the other was swollen and blank.

The figure glowed and shimmered. It leaned closer to the group and moaned, "Turn back." Its voice was as cracked and broken as its body. "Turn back!"

Minutes later, the kids were gathered in the lower lounge with Jenn. Raz sat on the couch and leaned against her.

Jenn wasn't his mother, but Raz had gotten used to being comforted by her. Dr. Mack was often busy with station business, like right now.

As soon as the group went through the lower level entrance, Dr. Mack and Skot had left to find Dr. Moors. His ship had landed in the docking bay at four that morning. Together they would investigate the weird happenings in the tunnel.

"It was a ghost!" Donnell said, pacing the lounge. Raz wasn't sure if his older friend was excited or terrified or a little of both.

As for the ghost, if that was what it was, it had disappeared as suddenly as it had appeared.

"Sweetie, sit down," Jenn said. "You're making Raz nervous."

Donnell snorted. "Raz doesn't need any help feeling nervous."

"I'm fine," Raz said. It wasn't true, but he didn't blame Donnell for his nerves. He blamed the ghost for that. Besides, he wasn't about to let Donnell know how scared he really was.

"Anyway, it wasn't a ghost," Kiley said.

"Right," Jenn added. "You remember what Skot said. The holographic projectors are broken. What we saw was a 'torn' projection of Jeeves."

"It didn't look like Jeeves," Raz said.

"He had a mustache," Kiley pointed out. "And he sounded like Jeeves."

"But if it was just a torn projection, why was he saying, 'Turn baaaaaack'?" Donnell asked. He used a deep and spooky voice. "'Tuuuuurn baaaaaack!'"

"Well, it doesn't matter whether that thing was Jeeves or a spirit," Kiley argued. She turned to Raz. "Either way it can't hurt us. It can't even touch us."

Raz wasn't so sure. No one *really* knew what a ghost could or couldn't do. A ghost might be able to suck his breath away or possess his body or some other horrible thing.

Before Raz could respond to his sister, the lounge doors whooshed open. Skot came in.

"Dr. Moors and I have been up and down the Art systems in lower engineering," he said. "There's nothing wrong with the holograms that we can see."

"So it *was* a ghost!" Donnell said.

"What?" Skot said. "Don't be ridiculous. I'll have to check the projector in the main tunnel. The problem must be at that end."

Raz curled in tighter to Jenn. A problem with *any* station part was unsettling. They hadn't even been in the lower level for one day. How could he take weeks of this?

"First, though," Skot went on, "let's go meet Dr. Moors and take a tour. Who's ready?"

Skot clapped his hands and stepped out the door. Raz wasn't eager to follow, but he got up anyway. The kids and Jenn hurried after Skot.

✦ ✦ ✦

"Ah!" Dr. Moors said. He stood outside the silver doors of lower engineering with Raz's mom. "There you all are."

Dr. Moors was an older man and quite short. He was only about Raz's height. That meant he was shorter than even Kiley and Donnell.

He wore glasses, which was unusual enough. Most people with poor vision either got lenses implanted or their eyes "fixed."

But Dr. Moors wasn't wearing simple glasses. His were made up of a dozen lenses, and each one was a different size and thickness. With the flick of a finger, the doctor could flip the lenses and change the strength of his glasses. It let him read a tablet, examine a microchip, and find a distant star—all without changing his eyewear.

"Harlan, this is Jenn," Skot said, smiling at his wife. "And my son, Donnell."

"That can't be!" Dr. Moors said. He seemed truly confused. "In the last picture I saw, Donnell was just a baby."

"Time flies, doesn't it?" Jenn said. She stepped forward to shake the doctor's hand. "It's nice to finally meet you in person."

"I'm so sorry," Dr. Moors said. He folded his hands in apology, leaving Jenn's hand empty. "I missed the wedding."

"Thirteen years ago," Skot pointed out.

"My, my," Dr. Moors said. "It's alarming what a man thinks of at the end of his life."

Raz looked at Kiley as if to say, *What's that supposed to mean?* His sister shrugged.

"And Dr. Mack," Dr. Moors said, "these must be your twins."

Kiley smiled brightly. Raz only managed a half-hearted wave.

"Now, let's go take a look around," Dr. Moors said. He turned to Skot. "If you don't mind, I'd love to give the tour. Test my memory a bit."

Skot gestured for Dr. Moors to lead the way. The older man launched into a speech about the lower level's various features as they headed down the hall. Dr. Moors had been part of the station's original design team. He seemed excited to show off his work.

The adults listened carefully. The twins and Donnell followed at the back of the group.

"The corridors are so narrow down here," Raz said. "It seems like the walls are closing in."

"That's just an illusion," Donnell said. He went to a wall and counted aloud as he walked across the corridor. "See? It's four meters, just like above."

"Well, it feels smaller," Raz said.

"It must be because there aren't any windows," Kiley said. "I feel closed off in here. The air is so stuffy."

"Yes, you're correct," Dr. Moors called to the kids. "Outside of engineering, no one has been down here in a long, long time. Most of the life support has been off for years."

He went back to talking with the other adults.

"I didn't think they were listening to us," Raz whispered to his sister.

"Yeah, that was strange," Kiley agreed.

Donnell jabbed Raz with an elbow. "Maybe Dr. Moors has weird gear in his ears too," he said. "Just like on his eyes."

Dr. Moors's quarters were close to engineering, but the families' suite was on the far side of the lower level. After a few minutes, Dr. Moors stopped in front of a wide door. Inside was a large living room with a food station and a bathroom. Opening up to this common area were three bedrooms.

"That means," Jenn told the kids, "you three will be sharing a room while we're down here."

"Yes!" Donnell said. He slapped a high five with Kiley and Raz.

Raz rubbed his hand and sighed. He had always shared a room with Kiley, but he wasn't sure Donnell would make a great roommate. After all, he'd been excited about the ghost. What if he played tricks to scare Raz even more?

✦ ✦ ✦

That night, Raz had a hard time getting to sleep. He had talked with Donnell and Kiley for an hour, then with Kiley for another hour after Donnell fell asleep. But still he lay wide awake in the darkened room.

When Raz finally did close his eyes, a face drifted to the front of his mind. It was that ghost—or Jeeves. Raz quickly opened his eyes to make it vanish.

But it didn't vanish. The face seemed to float above him. Its mouth hung open, and its voice droned like the air filtration system that hummed quietly in every room of the station.

"Please," Raz whispered, "leave me alone."

It didn't go away. It droned on, *Turn back. Turn back. Turn back.*

"Leave me alone," Raz said, louder now.

The torn face screamed, its voice like a wailing siren, *Turn back! Turn back!*

Raz yelled, "Leave me alone! Go away!"

"Raz, wake up!" the face replied.

Raz opened his eyes. Kiley was looking down at him, and the siren wailed on.

"What's going on?" Raz asked, dazed. Had he been dreaming?

"The station alarm is going off," Kiley said. "Something's wrong."

Raz jumped from his bed. The alarm was loud and sharp and cut right through his confusion.

"Come on, Raz," Kiley said, running toward the door.

"Where's Donnell?" Raz asked.

Kiley didn't answer. She stopped just inside the living room. Raz stopped beside her.

The living room was dark and quiet. Raz could barely see the outline of Donnell standing in front of them.

"Why isn't the alarm going off in here?" Raz asked. "I don't hear it at all anymore."

"I guess it must be over," Kiley said.

"Then where are our parents?" Donnell asked, turning to Raz and Kiley. He pointed to the other two bedrooms. Their doors stood open, and inside both were empty beds.

"They must have gone to check on the alarm," Kiley said.

"And left us here alone?" Raz said. He shook his head. "Jenn would have stayed behind. She always does."

The kids had gone through alarm drills before. They were always supposed to gather in the community living space. Jenn or station staff would meet the kids and lead them through the next steps. Except the three kids were already in the living room. So where were the adults?

"Well, my mom isn't here now," Donnell said. "I'm going to look for her."

"I don't think that's a good idea," Raz said. "There was an alarm. Something's wrong. We should wait here."

"We don't have time for this!" Donnell said. "I'm leaving!" With that, he ran to the doors. They whooshed open for him, but he stopped in the doorway.

Jenn was standing in the dimly lit corridor. Her back was to the kids, and she glowed blue in the low light.

"Mom?" Donnell said. "What's going on?"

Jenn didn't reply. She didn't even turn around. Instead she took off running.

"Mom!" Donnell called. He rushed into the corridor after her.

"Where is she going?" Kiley asked, sticking her head out the doorway.

"Come on," Raz said. He no longer wanted to wait there. Now he knew where Jenn was, and he knew she'd take care of them.

He dashed out the door and after Donnell and Jenn. Kiley was right behind him.

The corridors of the lower level were as dark as their suite had been. Only the glowing red emergency lights along the floor and the blue computer panels lit their way. Every screen they passed was locked, flashing the warning EMERGENCY IN PROGRESS.

Raz and Kiley caught up with Donnell quickly. But no matter how hard the three of them pushed, they never caught up with Jenn.

"She's not even running," Donnell said, barely with enough breath to speak.

He was right. Raz spotted her as they rounded a bend. She was walking down the far end of the hallway.

"Mom!" Donnell called as she vanished around the corner.

Raz sprinted as hard as he could, even keeping up with Donnell and Kiley. The three turned the corner, and Jenn was already thirty meters ahead.

She stood at the doorway to lower engineering. The doors opened, and she finally looked back. The kids stopped short and stared.

Jenn gave her typical warm smile as she looked at the kids and stepped into engineering. The doors whooshed closed behind her.

"What is she doing?" Donnell said. His voice cracked a little. For once he seemed as scared as Raz felt.

"Let's find out," Kiley said. She sprinted into engineering and the boys followed.

The doors slid open for them. Raz expected to find Jenn inside, and probably his mother, Skot, and Dr. Moors. All of them would be there, dealing with whatever emergency had set off the alarm.

But engineering was empty.

"What is happening?" Raz muttered, taking a step back from the open doorway.

The big room wasn't just empty. Engineering was as dark as the rest of the station, and the equipment inside looked as if it hadn't been used in years, maybe even decades.

Displays were cracked. Cables dangled from the ceiling and walls. The chief engineer's seat lay on its side, its bolts ripped from the floor.

Slowly, the children moved through the huge room.

"Mom?" Donnell called every few minutes. No one replied.

Raz looked over the dark panels. He wondered what each one did—or what each one had done when they worked.

"I don't get it," Kiley said from behind him.

Raz jumped. "Don't do that!" he snapped.

"Don't do what?" Kiley snapped back.

Raz crossed his arms and felt his face go hot. "Sneak up on people."

"Sorry," Kiley said. "But look. The place is a mess. Skot and Dr. Moors were in here earlier to check on the Art systems, right? So what were they doing? Nothing is even working."

Raz shrugged. He didn't understand anything that was going on right now.

"Mom?" Donnell called again.

Raz spotted Donnell across the room. He was wandering into the storage area. The door had rusted open. Donnell's voice echoed from the empty space beyond.

Then, out of the corner of his eye, Raz saw something. It was little, yellow, and flashing.

"What was that?" he said, turning quickly. But everything was dark.

"I saw it too," Kiley said.

Raz let his sister lead him toward where they thought they'd seen the flickering yellow light. When he stared hard into the darkness, he didn't see it. But if he let his eyes wander, he found it right away.

"It's there," Raz said, pointing to his right.

"Where?" Kiley said. "You're looking one way and pointing another."

"I know," Raz said. "I can't see it straight on, but when I look at it sideways, I can see it just fine. This way."

Kiley tried it too, and together they found the light. It flashed weakly from a communications panel.

The glass was splintered, and the flickering image was difficult to make out. Then a sound came crackling through.

"My ship is breaking up!" a voice said.

"It's Dr. Moors!" Raz said.

"Are you sure?" Kiley asked.

Raz shushed her so they could listen.

The voice sounded far away, and it faded in and out. "Repeat, we are breaking up," the voice said. It was definitely Dr. Moors. "Do not enter the—"

Suddenly the voice was cut off. The screen shattered. Raz shrieked as he and his sister shielded their faces from the shards of glass.

5

Raz and Kiley stood in the hallway just outside engineering. Raz struggled to catch his breath.

"Am I bleeding?" he asked, rubbing his face. He was certain the glass had torn it to bits.

Kiley shook her head. "No," she said. "Am I?"

Donnell burst out of engineering. "What happened to you two?" he asked. "You ran out of there like the place was on fire."

"Didn't you see?" Raz said. "Or hear?"

"What do you mean? Hear or see what?" Donnell asked. Kiley quickly told him about Dr. Moors's message.

"That doesn't make sense. Dr. Moors is on the station," Donnell said. "Why would he be sending a message?"

"Maybe he's not on the station anymore," Raz said. "We don't know where any of the adults are."

Donnell and Kiley both gave him a wide-eyed, anxious look. Without another word, the three sprinted back to their quarters.

✦ ✦ ✦

The wide door slid open with a whisper. Inside, the lights were on and Jenn, Skot, and Dr. Mack stood together in the living room. Their suitcases sat on the floor beside them.

"There you three are," Jenn said.

"*Us* three?" Donnell said. "Where have *you* three been?" He ran toward his dad, but Skot stepped to the side and picked up his bags.

"Dealing with the alarm, of course," Skot said.

"I hope you weren't scared," Jenn added.

Raz stood with Kiley near the door. He was so glad to see his mom and Jenn. But something felt . . . off.

"Why did you run away from us in the halls?" Raz asked Jenn.

She gave a tight-lipped smile. "Go get packed," she said, ignoring Raz's question. "We're heading back to the surface."

"The surface?" Raz said. He turned to his mom. "Aren't we still in the radiation band?"

"Does this have something to do with the alarm?" Kiley asked.

Dr. Mack stood up straighter, lifted her chin, and clasped her hands. The motion was familiar to Raz, but he couldn't quite place it.

"Of course," she said. "The radiation band is not nearly as dangerous as I predicted."

Raz glanced at Kiley.

"That is," Skot added, "it's not dangerous at all." He laughed. "You know how your mother has a way with words. Now, go pack your things."

"If you say so, Dad," Donnell said.

Raz and Kiley followed Donnell into their room. All three adults smiled at them.

"You guys," Donnell said as the door closed, "something very weird is going on."

"I know," Raz said. "Why would an alarm mean we're going back to the surface? Isn't an alarm usually bad news?"

"And why are they acting like everything is fine?" Kiley added. "Jenn was being weird, and engineering was falling apart. That's not normal."

The door slid open. "Come on, kids," said Jenn. "Just shove your stuff in a bag and let's go."

The adults led the children through the corridors toward the lower level's main exit. Although the corridors had been dark not long before, they were now brightly lit. Computer panels along the way were up and humming.

"What about Dr. Moors?" Raz asked from the back of the pack. "Isn't he coming up to the surface too?"

"No, his permanent quarters are down here," Skot said. "But there's no reason for us to stay down in this dark, musty place longer than we need to."

They reached the main door. It was the same door they'd sealed shut less than twenty-four hours ago. They had planned to leave it sealed for the next few weeks, at least. But here they were.

"My hands are full," Dr. Mack said at the front of the group. She was loaded down with two duffels and a case of science equipment. "And I don't even know where my pass card is in all this stuff."

"We've got the same problem," Jenn said. She glanced at Skot. His arms were also full.

"Hey, I know," Skot said, turning to smile at Donnell. "Son, why don't *you* unseal the door and let us all through?"

"Me?" Donnell said. He looked confused. "I don't have a pass card."

"Why not?" Skot asked.

"Because . . . only the senior staff members have them," Donnell replied.

"Yeah," Raz added. "Jenn doesn't even have a card."

"And you three," Jenn said, "are not senior staff members?"

"Um," Raz said. His stomach started to twist. *Why are they asking such weird questions?* he thought. Out loud he replied, "Of course not."

Jenn's smile fell into a frown. Skot's grin bent into a snarl, and Dr. Mack's face twisted in rage. The three adults all dropped their bags. Then they dove for the children.

As the grown-ups moved, they began to glow bright blue. Their bodies shimmered and shifted and grew larger. The adults started to blend together until they formed one giant, computerized face. It raised over the kids, its mouth fixed in a terrible scowl. Then it shrieked.

Donnell stumbled back. Kiley screamed.

Raz closed his eyes and covered his ears. He wanted to block out his mother's warped voice. But it roared in his ears, screaming wordlessly in anger and anguish.

Raz held his breath. He kept his eyes closed tight against the nightmare that had just come to life before him.

"It's OK," Kiley said. She pulled his hands from his face. "It's gone."

"Gone?" Raz said.

He opened his eyes. He, Kiley, and Donnell stood near the sealed door that led back to the surface. The hallway was dark aside from the blue light of a nearby control panel. And it was empty.

There was no enormous, angry face. No adults, who had suddenly turned from familiar and kind to warped and frightening. They were all gone.

Raz let out a ragged breath. The terror was over. But then it struck him that something was very wrong on the station—and they still didn't know where the adults were.

"So then where's Mom?" Raz asked.

"And where are my parents?" Donnell added. "Let's get back to—"

"There you are!" came a voice. Raz turned to see Jenn running toward them. She wrapped her arms around all three kids.

Raz stiffened for a moment. What if this Jenn was fake too? But her warmth made him relax. It had to be her.

"They're here!" Jenn shouted.

Raz heard footsteps as his mom and Skot rounded the bend in the hall. They rushed over.

"Oh, my darlings," Dr. Mack said, pulling Raz and Kiley into a hug. "What are you kids doing? We've been worried sick!"

"Jenn woke up and found your room open and empty," Skot said.

"Not to mention all of your stuff was missing," Jenn said. She nodded at the three duffel bags.

"We've had a pretty weird night," Donnell said.

"Come back to the suite," Dr. Mack said. She held Raz's hand tightly. "And tell us all about it."

Back at the suite, the two moms sat with their kids on the L-shaped couch in the living room. Skot paced the floor, going over the kids' story.

"It all had to be holograms," he said. "Even if you three had the same nightmare, which is impossible, how could you end up in the hall with your bags packed?"

"Group somnambulism?" Dr. Mack said.

"What?" Raz asked.

"Sleepwalking," Jenn explained.

"Also impossible," Skot said.

"So the people we saw were like Jeeves and Abigail?" Kiley asked. "But why are you three even in the system as holograms?"

"We aren't," Skot said. "But Art has access to security cameras, vocal records, personnel files—"

"That's it!" Raz said, remembering how familiar his fake mother's manners had been. "Mom wasn't acting like Mom. She was acting like Jeeves!"

"Ah," Skot said. "That makes sense. Art could have used images of Dr. Mack and recordings of her voice along with Jeeves's personality matrix to create a new character."

"Dad," Donnell said. "That explains just a little. Where were you three?"

"We were here worrying about all of you!" Jenn said.

"But when we left the first time, there was no one here," Kiley said. "The rooms were empty."

Skot fell into a chair. "That I can't explain," he said. "Art can do a lot with holograms, but it can't take away things. It can only add to a room or make it look different."

"So it can't erase whole people?" Donnell said.

"No way," Skot said.

"Unless . . . ," Raz said. He turned to look at the open doors to the adults' bedrooms. "Now that I think about it, we didn't actually go into your rooms. We just looked in from out here."

"What difference does that make?" Donnell asked.

"If the doors were closed," Raz said, "then Art wouldn't need to make anything disappear."

Skot's frown deepened.

"But they weren't closed," Donnell said. "We all looked inside and saw the rooms were empty."

"Maybe you didn't," Skot said. "If the doors were closed, Art could project a 3D image onto them. That way it would *look* like they were open and the rooms were empty. And the whole time we'd be inside, sleeping."

"But why would Art do that?" Jenn asked.

"Or any of this?" Kiley added. "It doesn't make sense."

"No, it doesn't," Skot said. "But the radiation band might be having any number of effects on Art's programming. I'll meet with Dr. Moors about it in the morning. Don't worry. In any case, no matter how odd the holograms act, they can't touch you or hurt you. We'll figure it out."

It all made sense to Raz, though. As he lay in bed that night, he couldn't shake a horrible thought: For some reason, Art was trying to get rid of the human crew.

7

Raz woke to everything shaking.

Actually, only he was shaking—because Kiley was shaking him.

"They're missing again, Raz!" she said.

"What?" Raz said, sitting up. He had a vague memory of a very bad dream.

"Mom, Jenn, and Skot!" Kiley said. "They're gone, but for real this time. Donnell and I went into their rooms to make sure. Donnell ran off to find them."

Raz's throat tightened. *Is this some new nightmare?* he thought.

As soon as Raz slipped out of bed, the twins sprinted through the empty morning corridors. At least, Raz was pretty sure it was morning. The hallway lights were on. The computer panels showed the time was 9:34 a.m.

But after last night, how could he be sure of anything? It was hard to know what Art was capable of in the radiation band. Turning on some lights and changing the clocks would be a cakewalk compared to creating fake holographic parents.

"There he is!" Kiley shouted.

Raz caught sight of Donnell as the older boy disappeared around the corner.

Oh no, Raz thought. *It's just like with Jenn last night!*

But this time, they caught up to Donnell. He had just reached the mess hall. At the same moment, the mess hall doors slid open.

The smell of pancakes and bacon drifted into the corridor. In the center of the bright room sat Skot and Jenn Prince, Dr. Moors, and Dr. Mack at the big, circular table.

"Oh," Donnell said. "You guys are . . . eating breakfast."

"That is what most people do in the morning," Skot said with a wink.

"We wanted to let you sleep in," Jenn said. She sipped her coffee. "You had quite a night."

"We were terrified!" Raz said. "We thought something had happened to you!"

"I should have left a note," Jenn said. "I'm sorry."

"We've been telling Dr. Moors all about your adventure," Dr. Mack said.

Raz looked at the old doctor. Though Skot was right that most people did eat breakfast, it seemed Dr. Moors did not. He had no food in front of him.

"Yes," Dr. Moors said. "I believe—"

"Aren't you hungry, Dr. Moors?" Raz asked.

"Raz!" his mom said. "You just interrupted Dr. Moors. That's very rude."

Raz felt his face grow warm. "Sorry," he said.

"It's quite all right," the doctor said. "I rarely eat breakfast. I don't have much of an appetite until I've done a full morning's work in the lab."

"I remember that," Skot said, setting down his fork. "But you did brew the best cup of coffee I've ever had. Do you want me to get you any?"

The doctor smiled and coughed into his hand. "No, no coffee," he said. "I had to, uh, give it up. It made me jittery."

"What were you saying about last night?" Kiley said as the kids sat at the table. "Did you find out anything?"

"Ah, yes, thank you," Dr. Moors said. "It seems to me that the issues we've been having with Art can all be explained by—"

"We?" Raz repeated.

"Raz!" Dr. Mack said. "Again?"

"Sorry, Mom," he said. "Excuse me, Doctor, but did something happen to you last night too?"

"Yes, as a matter of fact," Dr. Moors replied. "It was some minor holographic error. What's his name . . . the butler. Is it Geoffrey?"

"Jeeves," Skot corrected him.

"Yes, that one," the doctor said. "Jeeves. He suddenly appeared in my quarters and acted quite odd. But as I said, it was just a minor error."

"Minor?" Raz said. His heart raced as he remembered the terrible night. "What happened to us was *not* minor. The holograms tried to lead us up into the radiation. We could've died!"

"It's all right, Raz," Kiley said, putting a hand on his shoulder. "We never could have unlocked the door. Dr. Moors just means—"

"No, no, the boy is right," Dr. Moors said. He adjusted his strange glasses and looked into the distance. His eyes seemed to shrink. "These things can be very troubling, especially to children."

Kiley stared at him. "*Anyone* would've been upset by it."

The doctor went on as if he hadn't heard. "On Jupiter Station a few years ago, we had a similar issue," he said. "A bug in the holograms caused all sorts of images to appear randomly. Several of the younger residents found it very frightening indeed."

Raz crossed his arms. "We're not babies," he mumbled to Kiley. She nodded. Donnell sat silently, staring at the doctor.

"But there's no need to be afraid. Because I've found the problem," the doctor said, setting his glasses back to normal. "It's the radiation band that is causing the malfunctions."

Skot nodded. "As I suspected," he said.

"I studied the data from last night," Dr. Moors continued. "I have discovered that the radiation has a wavelength that is safe for life-forms such as yourselves. Ourselves, that is."

"Wait," Dr. Mack said, looking up. "Did you say . . . the radiation band is *safe*?"

"Exactly," Dr. Moors said. "Unless you happen to be a computer. I suggest the six of you pack your things and return to the surface. There's no need to be stuck down here."

"I'm sorry, Dr. Moors, but I have to disagree," Dr. Mack said. "All my weeks of research, data, and study tell me differently. I'm *certain* the radiation is dangerous."

"You are mistaken," Dr. Moors replied. "Simply put, to affect our computer system in the way that it clearly does, the radiation cannot possibly be of a wavelength that will harm humans."

"*I'm* mistaken?" Dr. Mack said, clenching her fork. "I'd like to see your data from last night."

"Mom," Kiley said. "At least finish breakfast."

"I don't have an appetite, and I don't suppose Dr. Moors does either," Dr. Mack said. She stared daggers at the man.

"Quite right," Dr. Moors said, apparently not noticing Dr. Mack's fury. "I'll be happy to go over the raw data. You'll find my sensors in lower engineering are superior even to yours."

Dr. Mack took a deep breath before replying, "Please, lead the way."

As the two scientists left the mess hall, Jenn and Skot stood too.

"Well, I guess they'll figure that out," Jenn said. "In the meantime you kids better get some food. I'll see you back at the suite for tutoring."

The Princes left, leaving the children behind.

"That was weird," Donnell said.

"Yeah, Mom was pretty mad," Kiley said.

"Dr. Moors was pretty rude," Raz replied. "He called us babies and called Mom stupid."

"Guys," Donnell said. "I'm not talking about your mom. I mean *Dr. Moors* was acting weird. Didn't you notice?"

Raz glanced at Kiley and then back at Donnell. "Notice what?"

"That he didn't eat," Donnell said.

"He said he never eats breakfast," Raz replied.

"He didn't have coffee," Donnell said.

"It makes him jittery," Kiley pointed out.

"He didn't drink any water or juice," Donnell went on. "He didn't touch a fork or a napkin or *anything* the whole time we were here."

Raz thought for a moment. "He touched his glasses," he said.

"Those are on his body," Donnell said. "I mean something that isn't connected to him."

"He was sitting in a chair," Kiley said. "So he touched the chair."

"Was he?" Donnell said. He went to grab the chair Dr. Moors had been sitting in—and his hand went right through it.

"It's a hologram!" Raz said. "So that wasn't Dr. Moors!"

"And Mom went with him!" Kiley said.

Donnell blew out a big breath. "I'll get my parents. You two go to engineering."

The kids dashed out of the mess hall. Donnell went left and the twins went right.

"It'll be OK," Kiley told her brother as they raced through the station. "A hologram can't hurt Mom."

Raz didn't say anything. They had to hurry. Because no matter what Kiley said, he knew that their mom was in danger.

8

The engineering doors slid open and Raz and Kiley hurried in. Raz heard a heavy clunk as the doors locked behind them.

Dr. Moors—or not—stood at the main control panel. He was staring through a huge window into a room beyond. Their mother was nowhere to be seen.

"Where is she?" Raz demanded as he stormed up to Dr. Moors.

The doctor turned. "Who?" he asked.

"Our mom," Kiley said, standing beside her brother. "Dr. Mack!"

"Ah. Dr. Mack is on my ship," the doctor replied. He swiped his fingertips over the panel in front of him.

"*Your* ship?" Kiley said. "We know you're not the real Dr. Moors!"

"I am whoever I wish to be," he replied, his voice cold. "Right now I am Dr. Moors, and your mother is on my ship."

Raz looked through the window at the docking bay beyond. It was lit up now. Inside was a small shuttlecraft. On its side in bold lettering, it said JUPITER STATION 12X-C. Through the shuttle's main window, Raz spotted his mom.

She waved to him. She seemed fine.

"Your mother refused to see the truth in my data," Dr. Moors said. "But since my ship is shielded against the radiation, I offered to let her go out into the band and collect the data herself. I only want to help. End-user satisfaction is my main concern."

"Mom is launching?" Raz said. His mind spun. He knew something was wrong, but he couldn't put his finger on what. Or could it be that this hologram was actually trying to help? After all, it was true that the shuttle was shielded against radiation.

Dr. Moors reached toward the bay door controls. Raz quickly covered the panel with his hands.

"Is something wrong?" Dr. Moors asked.

"Don't open the doors," Raz replied.

"Raz," Kiley said.

"He's trying to hurt Mom somehow!" Raz said. "I'm sure of it."

The hologram of Dr. Moors looked at him and smiled.

"But you can't stop him from reaching the controls," Kiley said. "He's part of the computer system, remember? He *is* the controls."

Raz's skin felt like ice.

An alarm shrieked throughout engineering. A voice echoed in the room, saying, "Docking bay doors opening in thirty seconds. Begin depressurizing. All ships leaving the station, please check your life support."

"There's no need to worry," Dr. Moors said. "She's quite safe aboard my ship."

"Your ship . . . ," Raz whispered to himself. "That message."

The nagging feeling finally made sense. Raz remembered the message clearly: *My ship is breaking up. Repeat, we are breaking up.*

"That's not Dr. Moors's ship, Kiley," Raz said. He turned to his sister. "His ship was damaged beyond repair before it even arrived on the Rock."

Kiley's face went pale. "But then this whole time, the real doctor was never even aboard the station!" she said. "And Mom . . ."

"Is about to run out of air very fast with only a broken shuttle protecting her," Raz said. "We have to get her out of there!"

Raz and Kiley stepped right through the hologram of Dr. Moors. Raz frantically started tapping the control panel.

"I think you'll find all the controls are locked," said Dr. Moors calmly. "I am sorry, but I will eliminate the human life-forms until full station control is returned to the computer. You—wait, what's happening?"

The doctor fizzled and cracked. Then he vanished before their eyes. The alarm stopped.

A moment later, Dr. Moors reappeared. But this doctor looked different. He didn't have a blue-ish tinge. He was see-through and tinted yellow. His odd-looking glasses were broken. His hair was messy, his clothes were ripped, and his face was covered in bloody scratches.

"Finally. Now, let's save your mother," Dr. Moors said to Raz and Kiley, and he grinned.

9

"I've gotten the better of that machine," said the dreadful-looking Dr. Moors. "But I don't know how long I can hold it off."

"Who—what . . . ?" Raz said.

"Please, I'm here to help, but you must hurry," Dr. Moors said. "Look."

The kids looked out into the docking bay. There was no gleaming shuttle from Jupiter Station. It was just a heap of metal with cracked windows, broken wings, and a dented hull.

Their mom sat in the pilot's seat and struggled with the hatch, trying to get out.

"I stopped the bay doors from opening, but I cannot open the ship for your mother," Dr. Moors said. "It won't take long for Art to regain control."

"Why should we trust you?" Kiley asked. "Dr. Moors never made it to the station. You're just another hologram!"

"I am not part of this station's computer system," the image said. "I am Dr. Moors."

"But the real Dr. Moors is—" Raz started to say, then stopped himself.

The image of the doctor nodded slowly. His see-through eyes looked tired, and his mouth curved into a frown that showed a depth of sadness Raz had never seen before.

Raz took a breath. "I believe you," he said.

"*What?*" Kiley said.

Raz ignored her. "What do we have to do?"

"Enter the tunnels beneath engineering," Dr. Moors said, "and disconnect Art. It's the only way to gain full control of the station. Follow me."

The eerie image floated across the room and stopped at a hatch. "Here," he said. "It's quite tight down there. It's one of the reasons my small size made me suited to the job."

"I'll have to go," Raz said.

"Alone?" Kiley asked.

Raz's heart thudded in his chest. "Yes, I can do it."

Kiley began to protest, but then Raz opened the hatch. They looked down into the tunnel, and they both knew Raz was the only one who could fit.

"Quickly now," Dr. Moors said.

Raz nodded. He took a deep breath, clenched his teeth, and climbed down the ladder into the dark, cramped tunnels.

It was cold. Raz remembered how the corridor leading into the lower level was only heated to a minimum to save energy. Raz guessed the same was true about these tunnels.

At the bottom of the ladder, Raz stood in darkness. "Is there a light down here?" he called. His voice echoed all around him, through tunnels in every direction.

"I will try to turn them on," Dr. Moors replied. "But you must hurry. Go down the tunnel to your right. There will be a thick cable running along the wall at your left. Follow it to the end."

"OK," Raz called back.

Feeling blindly in the dark, Raz found a tunnel opening and reached out with his left hand. There it was—a cable too thick for his hand to reach all the way around.

He walked forward, sliding his hand along the cable. It seemed to get darker as he went. His eyes ached with the strain of trying to see in the complete blackness.

"Any lights yet?" Raz called, but no reply came. He walked on.

"Stop at once, Raz Mack," said a familiar voice.

"Jeeves?" Raz asked, startled.

"Who else?" Jeeves replied. "I'm in the tunnel with you. You must turn around and return to engineering at once."

Raz shook his head. "You're trying to trick me."

He walked on, his hand on the thick cable.

"Are you frightened, Raz?" said a new and caring voice.

"Jenn?" Raz whispered. "I am scared. A little." His voice shook as he shivered in the cold. For an instant, his hand slipped from the cable and he nearly stumbled, but he got hold of it again.

"Come back to engineering," Jenn's voice said. "I'll make cocoa and you can warm up."

"No," Raz said. "You're not real."

He walked on. The tunnel seemed to go deeper as it curved through the belly of the science station.

"But *I'm* real, Raz," said his mother's voice. "And I'm still in the docking bay."

"I know," Raz said. "I'm going to save you."

"By leaving me there?" she replied. Anger rose in her voice. "I'm alone in the docking bay. You have to get me."

"No, Dr. Moors said—" Raz started to say.

His mom's voice cut him off. "Dr. Moors?" she snapped. "After all that's happened, do you *really* believe that was Dr. Moors? It was another of Art's tricks. Come back."

Raz stopped and held tight to the cable. Maybe she was right. Here he was, stuck in a cold, dark tunnel and getting farther and farther from his mom. Maybe that was just what Art wanted him to do.

"Raz!" someone else called. It sounded like Kiley. "Are you OK?"

Raz shook the voices from his head. "You're not real!" he shouted back.

"Um, you wish," Kiley replied. His sister's real voice cleared his head of the computer's terrifying impressions. "Are you almost at the end?"

"I—" Raz began, and he reached out. In front of him was a rough wall. One more step and he would have walked right into it. "Yes, I'm there!"

"Find the big switch and pull it from up to down," Kiley shouted. "That's all!"

Raz felt around for a switch. It was big all right. With both hands, he started to pull.

"Stop!" the voices screamed. It was every voice now. He heard his mom, the Princes, even himself.

The switch was heavy and sluggish. He continued to pull. The small tunnel began to grow hot—too hot. Uncomfortable. Raz felt like he might be cooked alive. Sweat rolled down his forehead.

"You must stop!" the voices shrieked at him.

Raz gritted his teeth and tugged the switch with all his strength as the voices screamed. The handle lowered and lowered . . . until it stopped with a thud and a click.

The voices went silent. A loud whirring filled the tunnel, and a moment later the lights switched on. The chamber became cooler immediately.

"Attention, station staff," a voice said over the station comm system. "The artificial intelligence has been shut down. All station systems are now under manual control."

Raz slumped against the side of the tunnel and sighed. "I did it."

Back in engineering, Raz climbed out of the tunnels. His sister, Donnell, Jenn, and Skot stood there waiting for him. They started applauding.

"Good job, Razzy!" Kiley said, throwing her arms around him.

Donnell patted him on the back. "That was pretty brave," he said.

"Where's Dr. Moors?" Raz asked.

"Gone," Kiley said. "I was lying down next to the hatch when the lights came on. I turned around and he had disappeared."

"And that's when the doors finally unlocked so my parents and I could get into engineering," Donnell said.

The door to the docking bay slid open.

"Mom!" Raz said. He ran to her.

"There he is," Dr. Mack said as she wrapped him in a hug. She was shaking slightly, but she was all right. "My hero."

Raz smiled.

"But I'm so confused," Dr. Mack added.

"I think the radiation was causing more than just system malfunctions," Raz said. "I think Art and the holograms were *trying* to hurt us."

Jenn looked at her husband. "Is that even possible?" she asked.

"It tried to get us to go back upstairs," Donnell said. "The holograms told us to turn back and wanted us to unseal the main door."

"It tried to suffocate Mom in the docking bay," Kiley added.

"And it tried everything to stop me from reaching the shutdown switch," Raz finished. He shivered at the memory. "It almost seemed like Art was trying to protect itself."

"I suppose it's not unheard of for artificial intelligence systems to develop wants and needs," Skot said. His face was wrinkled in worry. "One of the first systems used in space travel became obsessed with music. No one could figure out why. It wouldn't focus on anything else. It had to be shut down."

"Sounds better than an obsession with getting rid of all humans," Raz said.

Skot nodded. "We'll keep the system off-line until I can get to the bottom of this," he said.

"I still don't understand one thing," Kiley said. "What about the hologram of Dr. Moors, the one who helped us? Why would Art turn on itself like that?"

"That wasn't a hologram," Raz said. He went to the controls that looked out over the docking bay. Staring at the broken ship, he tapped the panel. "Computer, tell me the location of Dr. Moors."

"Dr. Harlan Moors is not on board the station," the computer replied.

Skot came up next to Raz. The concern on his face was deepening. "Computer," he said, "is Dr. Moors at Jupiter Station?"

"No," the computer replied. "Dr. Moors left Jupiter Station eighty-seven days ago."

"Sounds about right," Skot said. "Computer, when did Dr. Moors arrive at the Rock?"

"Dr. Moors did not arrive at the Rock," the computer replied. "Shuttlecraft Jupiter Station 12X-C was brought into the lower docking bay yesterday at four hundred hours by the automated tractor beam. It was heavily damaged. Dr. Moors was not on board and is presumed lost."

Skot fell back into the seat at the control panel, shock on his face.

"Dad?" Donnell said. "Are you OK?"

"Dr. Moors," Skot said. "He . . . he's dead."

The control panel glowed yellow for a moment, and then a familiar recording played.

STATUS:
Presumed
Lost

"This is Shuttlecraft Jupiter Station 12X-C," said Dr. Moors's voice. "I have no control of the ship. Onboard computer is malfunctioning. My ship is breaking up, and life support is failing. I will not reach Science Station: Rock. I repeat, we are breaking up. Do not enter the radiation band. It is too dangerous. Do not enter the—"

Raz felt Kiley's hand wrap around his. The kids and their parents said nothing for a long moment.

"I think it was him," Raz finally said. "I think it was the real Dr. Moors who helped us."

"Raz," Kiley said softly. "Not now."

"No," their mom said. "I think it's possible. In the radiation band, matter and energy are entirely unpredictable. There's so much to the universe we don't understand."

Raz nodded. "I think Dr. Moors's spirit managed to take control of the station away from Art."

"So that recording we heard . . . ," Kiley began.

"Dr. Moors tried to play it for us, to warn us. Just bits of it came through," Raz said.

"But he got better at reaching out," Kiley said, her eyes widening.

"Until he could appear and help us save Mom," Raz finished.

"I'm not sure," Skot said. He leaned forward. "What you're suggesting—it sounds more like the supernatural than the scientific."

But Raz and Kiley were sure. Only one thing could have saved them all from the station's artificial intelligence: the ghost of Dr. Moors.

SPACE RADIATION

Outer space isn't empty, although it may look that way. It's filled with radiation. On Earth we live with many types of radiation, but space radiation can be very harmful to humans and machines.

Radiation is made of invisible rays, waves, and super tiny particles called protons. These protons can zoom through a spacecraft or an astronaut without being noticed. They can break apart human cells or kill them. That causes serious health problems (such as memory issues, heart disease, or cancer) right away or over time.

Our sun is the closest source of space radiation. It releases bursts of charged particles. Some particles travel through space. Others get trapped in huge magnetic fields high above Earth and form the Van Allen radiation belts. Beyond Earth's orbit, space travelers are exposed to Galactic Cosmic Rays, or CGRs. This dangerous radiation comes from outside our solar system.

Astronauts going on faraway missions would be exposed to all three types of radiation. We can't yet fully protect humans or electronics from this invisible threat. But hopefully, the only tech issue future space explorers will have to worry about is slow response times—not a computer trying to kill them!

—Michael

GLOSSARY

artificial intelligence (ar-ti-FISH-uhl in-TEL-uh-junss)—a computer system with the ability to think like a person

asteroid (AS-tuh-royd)—a large space rock that moves around the sun

end user (END YOO-zer)—the person who uses a finished product, such as a machine or computer program

engineering (en-juh-NEER-ing)—the department that is focused on making sure the ship, and everything on it, is working correctly and in good condition

hologram (HOL-uh-gram)—a special type of image that looks solid and real, and is created with laser light

malfunction (mal-FUHNK-shun)—to fail to work correctly or normally

manual (MAN-yoo-uhl)—done by hand, not by machine

quarters (KWOR-turs)—a place where someone lives

radiation (ray-dee-AY-shuhn)—energy that is given off in the form of rays, waves, or particles; you cannot see radiation, and some types are dangerous to living things

ration (RASH-uhn)—food or supplies, often a particular amount that is given daily

ABOUT THE AUTHOR

Steve Brezenoff is the author of more than fifty middle-grade chapter books, including the Field Trip Mysteries series, the Ravens Pass series of thrillers, and the Return to Titanic series. He's also written three young-adult novels, *Guy in Real Life*; *Brooklyn, Burning*; and *The Absolute Value of -1*. In his spare time, he enjoys video games, cycling, and cooking. Steve lives in Minneapolis, Minnesota, with his wife, Beth, and their son and daughter.

ABOUT THE ILLUSTRATOR

Juan Calle is a former biologist turned science illustrator, trained at the Science Illustration program at California State University, Monterey Bay. Early on in his illustration career, he worked on field guides of plants and animals native to his country of origin, Colombia. Now he owns and works in his art studio, LIBERUM DONUM, creating concept art, storyboards, and his passion: comic books.